11-05

AR Quiz # 80373

Down Girl
and Sit

Down Girl and Sit

Smarter than Squirrels

by Lucy Nolan

Illustrations by Mike Reed

Marshall Cavendish

New York 🐾 London 🐾 Singapore

Marshall Cavendish
99 White Plains Road
Tarrytown, NY 10591
www.marshallcavendish.us

Library of Congress Cataloging-in-Publication Data

Nolan, Lucy A.
Down Girl and Sit : smarter than squirrels / by Lucy Nolan ;
illustrations by Mike Reed.— 1st ed.
p. cm.
Summary: Recounts the adventures of a rambunctious dog who thinks her
name is Down Girl and her next door neighbor, Sit, as they try to keep the
world safe from dangerous squirrels, the paper boy, and a frightening creature
named Here Kitty Kitty.
ISBN 0-7614-5184-6
[1. Dogs—Fiction. 2. Humorous stories.] I. Reed, Mike, 1951- ill. II. Title.

PZ7.N688Do 2004
[Fic]—dc22
2004001400

The text of this book is set in Garamond.
The illustrations were created in Corel Painter 8.

Book design by Adam Mietlowski

Printed in The United States of America

Marshall Cavendish Chapter Book, First edition

3 5 6 4 2

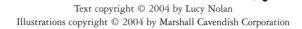

To Nutmeg and Becky, of course

—L.N.

To Jane, Alex, and Joe

—M.R.

Contents

Chapter 1
Smarter Than Squirrels   11

Chapter 2
I Ate It   24

Chapter 3
Follow Your Brain   37

Chapter 4
Dogs Don't Lie   51

Hamburger Man's house

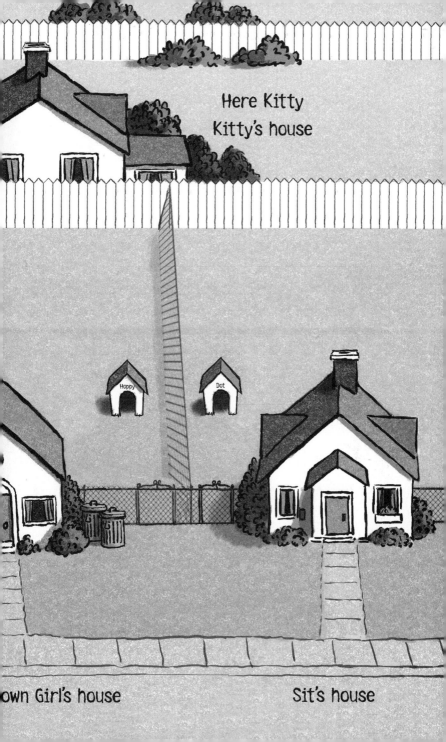

Chapter 1

Smarter Than Squirrels

Good morning. My name is Down Girl.

This is my neighbor. Her name is Sit.

"Hello, Sit."

"Hello, Down Girl."

We are very busy dogs.

Sometimes we move sticks from place to place. Sometimes we work in the garden. Sometimes we sing.

There is a fence between us, but it is a good kind of fence. We can talk to each other and touch noses through the wire. We like this kind of fence.

The back fence is a bad fence. It is hard to see through the boards. Still, we know what waits on the other side. Something lives there that is too horrible to talk about. We stay away from the fence and keep our wits about us.

That is a good thing. We never know when we'll have to spring into action. It is up to us to keep the world safe. Sometimes Sit and I wish we had help, but we've gotten used to doing the job alone.

The secret to our success is simple. We are smarter than squirrels.

I don't think people realize how many birds and squirrels are out here. If they did, they'd never leave their houses.

Birds and squirrels steal almost everything in sight. What they don't steal, they eat. They are very clever, but they are not as clever as we are. Guess where we chase them. We chase them up trees!

You never see a dog in a tree, do you? That's because dogs are smart. We know it would hurt to fall out.

Birds and squirrels never remember
this. It's easy to keep the world safe from
birds and squirrels. The other day we came
across something much worse.

Here's what happened.

It started like any other day. My master, Rruff, was sound asleep.

I stuck my nose into my water bowl. Then I touched Rruff to wake him up. I like to be the first thing he sees in the morning.

"Down, girl!" Rruff shouted.

"Rruff!" I answered, and wagged my tail.

"Down, girl!" he said again.

"Rruff!" I repeated more loudly. I don't think he hears very well.

Rruff is lucky I woke him when I did. In another hour the alarm clock would have gone off and scared him.

Next I ran to the front window. It was barely light outside. I knew the boy would be coming soon. He comes every morning.

I waited on the sofa. The boy was very quiet. I was very quiet too. I watched him. He pulled out a rolled-up newspaper.

I know what newspapers are for. They are for spanking. I jumped against the window. I barked and barked.

The boy dropped the newspaper and rode away. I laughed. Once again I had saved my master from getting spanked.

I trotted into the kitchen and found the doughnuts Rruff had set out for us. They were way up on the counter.

"Down, girl!" Rruff said.

I didn't answer with my mouth full. I wagged my tail to thank him. So far, the day was going smoothly.

Now it was time for our morning walk. We met Sit and her master. After a few blocks, we ran into our good friend Hush. Hush told us the big news. Something

horrible had moved onto our street. It was bigger than a squirrel and twice as ugly. Its name was Here Kitty Kitty.

This creature sounded like trouble, all right. Sit and I knew it was up to us to guard our masters' hiding places. This is where they bury everything that is dear to them. Chicken bones, soggy cereal, and lots of wonderful, stinky food.

Our masters keep their hiding places just outside the fence. They use them over and over. When will they learn to be smart like dogs? We bury our treasures all over the place. We bury our treasures in so many places, even we can't find them again. It's a brilliant plan.

Sure enough, Here Kitty Kitty came creeping around that afternoon. Sit hid in the bushes on her side of the fence. I hid in the bushes on my side of the fence. Here Kitty Kitty began to sniff around the hiding places. We sprang out of the bushes. Sit barked.

Crash! Rotten food flew into the air. So did Here Kitty Kitty.

Here Kitty Kitty jumped into my yard. I chased him. Guess where I chased him? I chased him up a tree!

I looked at Sit, and we smiled. What large brains we have!

We had Here Kitty Kitty right where we wanted him. We were so excited, we rolled in the spoiled tomatoes.

Here Kitty Kitty yawned, but we knew he was really afraid. Who could not be afraid of two dogs like us?

We knew what Here Kitty Kitty was

thinking. *Why did I run up this tree? Now I will be stuck up here forever.*

Well, just wait! We knew something he did not know.

We have chased lots of birds and squirrels up that tree. If Here Kitty Kitty did not fall out, surely they would push him out!

Here Kitty Kitty must have thought the same thing. He decided to climb out of the tree. I couldn't believe it! He must be smarter than squirrels.

But wait! Maybe he wasn't. He jumped onto the back fence.

"Not the back fence!" I shouted.

Here Kitty Kitty didn't listen. In fact, he laughed at me.

Suddenly a hand reached up and grabbed him! His eyes grew wild. Then he was gone.

The smell of roses drifted through the air.

Sit and I tucked in our tails and ran. We did this in a very cool way, of course.

"Is it . . . ?" Sit asked. "Did she . . . ?"

Sit couldn't bring herself to say the words. We both slunk to the fence and peeked. Oh, it was worse than we thought!

Bath!

Shampoo!

Perfume!

The smell of roses was strong.

We didn't get any on us, did we?

Sit and I quickly sniffed each other. Nope! We still stink!

Whew! That was a close call.

Sit and I looked at the fence and smiled. Sometimes help comes from the most unexpected places.

Chapter 2

I Ate It

I was in a good mood the next day. Sit trotted to the fence with a stick in her mouth. "You look fetching," I said.

Ha! I crack myself up.

As always, I was watching the squirrels. If I didn't do it, who would?

Rruff certainly wouldn't do it. Rruff is sweet, but he doesn't have a clue about what goes on around him.

Let me tell you what he did that morning. Rruff found a hard old doughnut on the counter.

Now, what is the normal thing to do? The normal thing is to eat it.

What did Rruff do? He broke it into little pieces. Then he put the pieces on the ledge outside the kitchen window.

Don't ask me why he did this. This is just the kind of thing he does.

I knew something he didn't know.

If he left that doughnut there, the birds would eat it. Then we'd never get rid of them. Rruff came back inside for our walk, and I squeezed past him.

I ran straight to the doughnut pieces.

I ate them.

"Down, girl!" Rruff shouted.

He sure was in a hurry for our walk.

I thought about that old doughnut all morning. I decided that there are a lot of good things to eat in our yard. If I got rid of all those things, the birds and squirrels might go away. When we got back from our walk, I looked carefully around.

Squirrels like acorns. There are a lot of acorns in our yard. I tried to bury most of them, but there were still a few left.

So I ate them.

The birds really like our garden. Perhaps

that's because the flowers are so beautiful.

So I ate them.

Sticks? Birds and squirrels build nests with them. I ate them.

Ferns? I ate them.

Garden hose, doormat, lawn chair? I ate them.

Well, okay, maybe I didn't actually eat all those things. A dog has to draw the line somewhere, but I did chew them up.

Then I had my most brilliant thought of all. I looked at the pole in the middle of the yard. Rruff puts seeds on top of that pole every day.

I know, I know. That is not a normal thing to do.

When he walks away, the birds eat the seeds. The squirrels do, too. If Rruff had any idea this was going on, he would stop doing it.

I tasted the seeds that were lying on the ground. They could use a little salt, but I ate them anyway.

I couldn't get to the seeds on top of the pole, but I knew where Rruff stored the rest. He goes into the shed every morning and brings out more. If I could get into the shed, I could get rid of the seeds. That would solve two problems at once. The birds and squirrels might leave, and Rruff could find a more useful hobby.

I crawled under the door of the shed. There was the bag of seeds.

That's not very big, I thought. I can eat that.

So I ate it.

And what was that? Was that a bag of my food? Yes, it was. I recognized the poodle on the front. He always seems so happy about the meaty taste.

The squirrels would never leave if they found my food. So I ate the whole bag.

When I was finished, I was stuffed. I had eaten all those things to save the world! That's just the kind of dog I am.

It was almost time for Rruff to come home. I thought I'd better crawl out to meet him.

But wait! Something was wrong. Somehow, while I wasn't looking, the space under the door had gotten smaller. I almost got stuck.

Maybe if I turned over, I thought, I could wiggle out on my back. This time I really did get stuck.

I was upside down. All of the squirrels were laughing at me. But I am still smarter than squirrels. How?

Hmm. Well, I will tell you how, as soon as I think of a reason.

Okay, here is why I am smarter than squirrels. I was in the shed and they were not. They couldn't get to the food because I was guarding it. Besides, there was no food for them to get to. I had eaten it.

It is very clear that I am smarter.

But how was I going to get free? There was nothing to do but whine. I whined in a very cool way, of course.

Finally, Rruff came home. He put his hands on his hips and stared down at me. I could see that he was proud of me for being such a good guard dog. I could also see straight up his nose.

Rruff tried to pull me out, but that didn't work. He tried to push me back inside. That didn't work either.

He disappeared for a few minutes. Then he came back with Sit's master. They took the whole door off the shed.

Rruff looked inside at the empty bags. He gave me a very sad, disappointed look.

Poor, sweet Rruff. He must have thought the birds and squirrels ate all of my food. Doesn't he know they are not that smart?

Rruff pointed his finger at me and started to shout. I know he was upset about the squirrels, but I wish he wouldn't yell so loud. That is not very attractive.

We went into the house. I lay down. Hmm, somehow my little rug had gotten smaller.

Rruff didn't pick up my food bowl like he usually does. He didn't even give me a snack. Instead, he fixed a salad for himself and sat down.

Eating and food. Is that all he thinks about?

The worst part is, he didn't even offer me any. Of course, dogs hate salad, but that is not the point.

Wait! Here is why Rruff didn't give me dinner. He wanted to give me dessert instead. He had set a whole pie right on the edge of the table.

"Down, girl!"

Rruff ran straight for me. But quite frankly, I was too full to be hugged. I ran the other way.

When life gives you pie, you should never stop to think. That's why I ended up behind the couch with the pie, some dust, and one old raisin.

Here's something odd. The couch had somehow gotten smaller, too. I went ahead and stretched out for the night behind it.

It had been a long day. Still, I found time to do one more important thing before I went to sleep.

I ate the raisin.

Chapter 3

Follow Your Brain

It's not easy being a dog. There are too many things to remember.

For instance, we have to remember that new shoes are not playthings. Bumblebees are not playthings either.

If we didn't have such large brains, we might become as forgetful as our masters.

The other day Rruff forgot to eat breakfast. I couldn't believe it. Rruff never starts the day without toast or a doughnut.

At least he put my coffee where I could reach it.

"Down, girl!"

"Rruff!" I love that man.

We met Sit and her master for our walk. When the walk was over, all four of us ended up in my backyard. Did Sit's master forget where they really lived?

Oh, well. Sit and I didn't say anything. We knew something our masters did not know. As soon as our leashes were off, we would play together in my yard. We ran around, chasing each other, while our masters smiled.

But wait! Our masters had somehow gotten out of the fence when we weren't looking. They were riding off on bicycles. Here's the worst part. They forgot us!

I jumped against the gate. I barked and barked. Suddenly the gate swung open. I actually opened the gate! I thought I was brilliant. Sit thought the gate was unlocked to begin with.

It didn't matter. Sit and I were free. We

could go after our masters!

I turned to Sit. "Should we walk or take the car?"

Ha! I am just too funny.

We saw which way our masters went. We ran in that direction. We put our noses to the ground and followed their trail. After three blocks, we began to lose the scent.

"It's time to quit following our noses and start following our brains," I said.

Where could our masters possibly be?

"Perhaps they stopped to roll in that leaf pile," Sit said. That was an excellent suggestion!

Sit and I trotted over to it. Our masters

weren't anywhere in sight. That didn't mean they weren't hiding down deep in the pile.

Sit and I sniffed it. We didn't smell Rruff. We could tell that a poodle, a collie and two cocker spaniels had been there. Quite frankly, the leaf pile stunk. We jumped right in.

If our masters had passed up this much fun, they must have gone somewhere even better. Where could that be?

"Perhaps they went to swim in the creek," I said.

That was another good idea!

Sit and I splashed all through the creek.

When we climbed out, we were covered with green pond scum.

"Ha!" I told Sit. "You look like a salad!"

We laughed and crept along, pretending to be salads. Then we remembered salads don't creep. They don't do anything at all. They just sit there. That kind of took the fun out of it.

Where else could our masters be? We were running out of places to look. It was time to think about this more deeply.

"If we weren't at home, where would we be?" I asked.

Finally the obvious answer hit us.

"We'd go to the park to chase squirrels!" we both shouted.

This was our best idea yet.

When we got to the park, our masters weren't there. We chased squirrels anyway. We didn't even do it to save the world. We did it just for fun.

After a while, Sit and I began to wonder if we would ever see our masters again. We were feeling very sad.

All of a sudden I caught the whiff of something familiar in the air. I quivered all over with excitement. I couldn't believe what my nose was telling me.

"Is it Rruff?" Sit asked.

"No!" I said. "It's a doughnut!"

Sit and I followed the scent. We went up one street and down another. Then we found the most amazing place. People were sitting and eating at tables outside. Doughnuts were everywhere.

Quite frankly, I'm surprised we were the only dogs there.

Then I saw Rruff. He was eating with Sit's master. We wagged our tails and ran to them.

"Down, girl!"

"Sit!"

Our masters did not seem happy to see us. We tried to leave, but they didn't want us to. I wish they'd learn to make up their minds.

Our masters invited us to lie down next to them. In fact, they insisted on it.

I was being good. I really was. Then I saw a man at the table next to us. He had a bag of doughnuts.

I did the only thing I could do. I inched my way over to him and begged. I did this in a very cool way, of course.

When you beg in a cool way, it is not called begging. It is called staring.

The man pulled out a newspaper. He pushed the bag of doughnuts to the edge of the table.

Why, thank you! What a generous man. "Down, girl!"

I looked up. Rruff was heading towards me. What? Was it time to go already?

Okay, I could finish my doughnuts on the way.

I ran between the tables. Rruff ran after me. The man did too. It was so much fun, I did it again. So did Rruff. Everywhere I ran, Rruff was right behind me. Why was he following me everywhere? That's when I figured it out. He must have forgotten how to get home by himself.

Thank goodness Sit and I knew the way.

We ran through the neighborhood. Our masters stuck close behind us on their bicycles. They were shouting the whole way. Were they afraid we would leave them behind?

It was hard to run with the doughnuts. I knew Rruff was depending on me to get him home. I kept going. I didn't even stop to chase squirrels in the park.

Okay, maybe I chased one or two.

When we got home, I ran through the open gate. I sat in the backyard to wait.

Rruff finally rolled up, huffing and puffing. Perhaps he should cut down on the doughnuts.

Sit and I ate the whole bag ourselves.

Then I ran to greet Rruff. He leaned against the house, panting. I kissed him.

"Down, girl!"

That's what I love about Rruff. He is very forgetful, but in the end he always remembers what's important. He remembers me. He remembers that I am his best friend in the world.

And even though he gets out of the fence from time to time, he always remembers to come home.

Chapter 4

Dogs Don't Lie

Yesterday I could feel danger the minute I woke up from my nap. No, wait. That wasn't danger. That was just the pinecone I was lying on.

But still, things hadn't felt right all day.

It all started when Rruff packed his bag. I don't like it when he does that. That means he will be away all night.

Rruff would leave me. I would starve.

Oh, all right, that's not true. Everyone knows dogs can't lie. I don't even know why I tried.

Rruff would have somebody come feed me. It could be Sit's master. It could be the man next door. He is not my favorite person. He grills hamburgers and never gives me any.

When I saw that bag sitting on Rruff's bed, I jumped inside. I hoped Rruff wouldn't see me.

"Down, girl!"

My trick worked. If he was calling me, he must not know I was right under his nose. I was so happy, I jumped out and kissed him. He snapped the bag shut.

Well, that didn't work out the way I had planned.

I hung my head and looked sad. I decided that I would never speak to Rruff again.

He patted my head.

Here's the problem with being so honest. My tail started wagging. I hate it when that happens.

I wanted Rruff to think I was mad at him. Then he would be too upset to leave.

I followed Rruff to the kitchen. He had his bag in one hand and a doughnut in the other hand. He opened the back door, but I wouldn't go out. If I didn't leave the house, neither would he.

He threw the doughnut out the door. I ran after it.

The door closed.

Rats! I didn't see that coming.

Rruff hugged me good-bye and drove away. I knew I would not see him again until tomorrow.

I wasn't about to let the squirrels know how sad I was. I spent the day chasing them. I also talked to Sit. Then I dragged flowerpots from one side of the yard to the other.

It was very important to keep a normal schedule. That's why I finally made myself take a nap. When I woke up, Sit had already gone inside. There I was, alone in the yard at supper time.

Here's the weird part. I felt as if someone was watching me.

Shhh!

I could hear the leaves rustling around the corner of the house. Somebody was coming to feed me.

Was it Sit's master? Was it the

hamburger man? Who could it be?

I couldn't believe it. It was Here Kitty Kitty!

Why would Rruff send Here Kitty Kitty to feed me?

Here Kitty Kitty headed toward the hiding places. He could not fool me. Rruff did not send him.

I barked and barked. Here Kitty Kitty ignored me. He tipped over one of the hiding places.

I knew this would happen one day. It is going to upset Rruff very much. One day he will want to eat some soggy cereal, and it will all be gone.

I was not worried. After all, I am the dog who can open gates! I jumped against the gate. It did not open this time. Then I had another brilliant plan. I could crawl under the gate. I remembered how easy it was to crawl into the shed.

Unfortunately, I forgot about how hard it was to crawl out of the shed. My nose got stuck under the gate.

Let's not tell Rruff that part of the story. Okay?

Here Kitty Kitty continued to pick through our treasures. I barked. Have you ever tried to bark with your nose stuck under a gate?

Here Kitty Kitty stopped to look at me. I guess he's never heard a dog say "Merf" before.

Suddenly I saw something horrible behind him. I froze. Well, actually, I couldn't move anyway, but that is not the point.

Here Kitty Kitty thought I was trying to trick him. He thought I was only pretending that something was behind him.

Doesn't he know that dogs don't lie?

Instead of running, Here Kitty Kitty sat there and laughed. A hand reached down and snatched him.

It was the girl from behind the back fence. She clutched Here Kitty Kitty to her chest. I pulled my nose free. I was so excited, I jumped up and down.

"Down, girl!"

There was a boy standing by the fence. He knew my name, but I didn't know his. He looked kind of familiar though. He started coming my way.

Uh-oh.

The little girl stayed where she was. She squeezed Here Kitty Kitty. The boy came through the gate. He was older than the girl, so they couldn't have come from the same litter. Maybe that meant he was not quite as crazy as she is.

I was not going to take any chances. The boy whistled for me. I didn't go to him.

What was this? He had my food bowl and my dinner!

I didn't want to look behind me. I felt sure my tail was wagging. Rats.

After I ate, the boy threw a stick. That made him look even more familiar.

He was still trying to win me over, but I wasn't going to get that stick.

Okay, I got that stick, but I wasn't going to let him pet me.

Well, okay, maybe I'd let him pet my head and my ears and my back.

I loved this boy. He was my new best friend.

But wait! The gate was squeaking. The girl was coming toward me with a baby doll.

Where was Here Kitty Kitty? What horrible thing had she done to him?

I wanted to run, but the boy was hugging me.

The girl reached into her pocketbook. What did she have in there? Was it soap? Or was it something even worse?

Oh no.
It was . . . a doughnut?

The little girl held out the doughnut.

I would not wag. I would not kiss her. I would ignore her.

Maybe I would ignore her after I ate the doughnut.

She scratched my ears while the boy rubbed my back.

That's when I knew everything was going to be okay. I would see Rruff tomorrow. I would have a good story to tell Sit. In the meantime I had everything else a dog needs. I had some good friends, a large brain and doughnut breath.

Then the little girl showed me her baby. It was wrapped up in a blanket. It was the ugliest baby I have ever seen.

It was Here Kitty Kitty in a bonnet.

I didn't even have to look behind me.

My tail was wagging. I knew it was.